Bears in Beds

Shirley Parenteau
illustrated by David Walker

WALKER BOOKS
AND SUBSIDIARIES
LONDON · BOSTON · SYDNEY · AUCKLAND

Five empty beds
are waiting there.
It's time to sleep.
Where are the bears?

Here comes sleepy
Big Brown Bear.
He climbs into bed.
He's happy there.

Now comes drowsy
Yellow Bear.
He takes the bed near
Big Brown Bear.

Fuzzy whirls in
like a circus bear.
She swirls into bed
with a twirly flair!

There's a blur of fur.
Is that a bear?

Yes!
It's Calico tumbling
with Floppy Bear!

"It's time to sleep!"
says Big Brown Bear.
He gets out of bed
to untangle that pair.

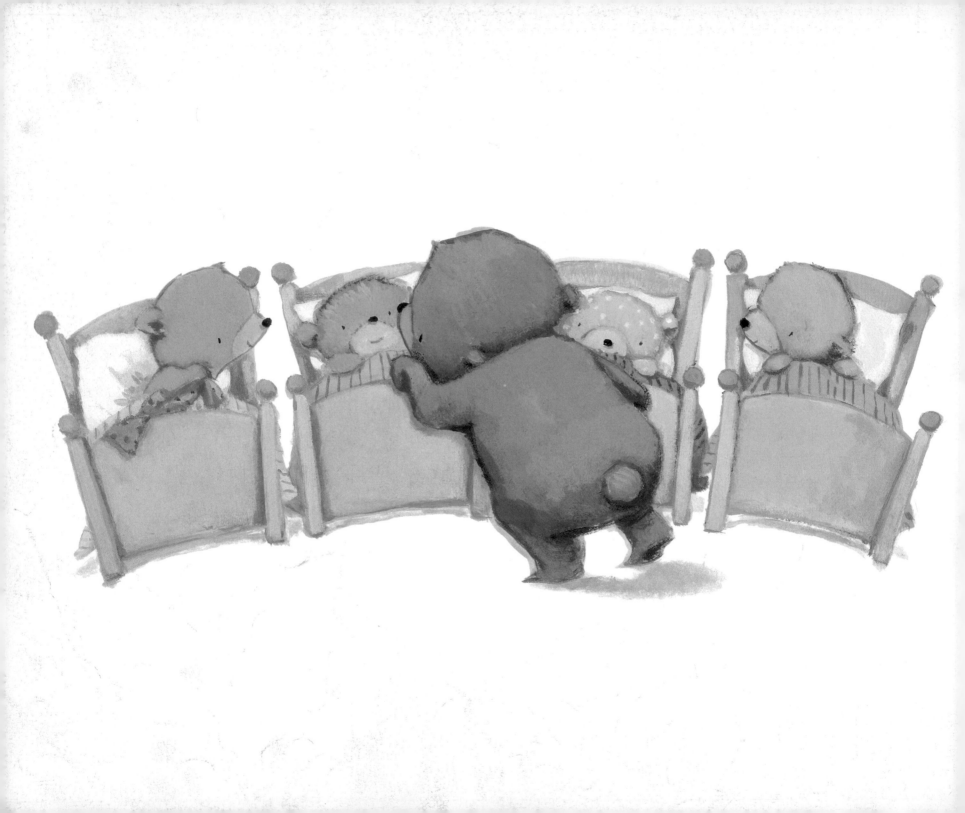

He tucks them in,
then Big Brown Bear
blows a kiss goodnight
to all four bears.

Out goes the light!
It's cosy in there.

Five warm beds
hold five tired bears.

Whoosh

goes a sound
in the middle of the night.
Big Brown Bear
wakes up in a fright!

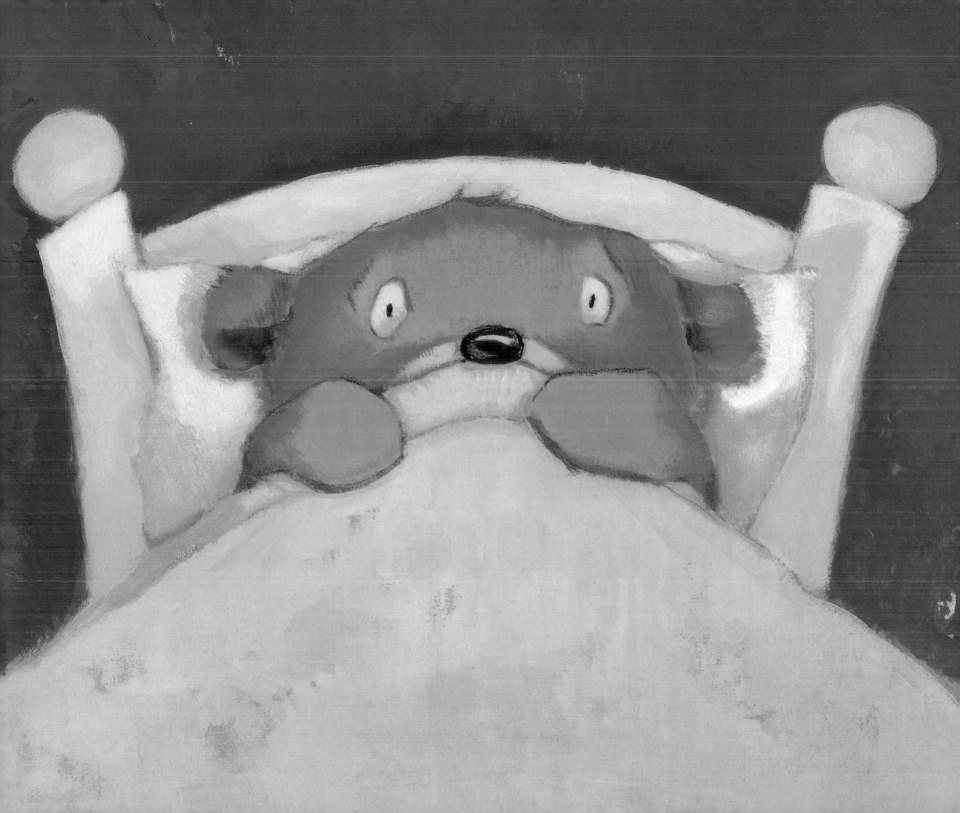

Whoosh! Whoosh! Whoosh!

Moans fill the air.
Is that the wind,
Big Brown Bear?

Oh, no!

Rattle, rattle, rattle
from under the chair.

He turns on the light
to see what's there.

It's Fuzzy, Yellow
and Calico Bear!
Floppy peers from
under the chair!

They heard the wind.
They had a scare.
They're afraid to stay
in their beds over there.

"Come snuggle close,"
says Big Brown Bear.
So the four little bears
scramble up there.

He reads them a story
about three bears
and a pesky girl
with golden hair.

Their eyes slowly close.
Soft snores fill the air
from one big bed full
of five sleeping bears.

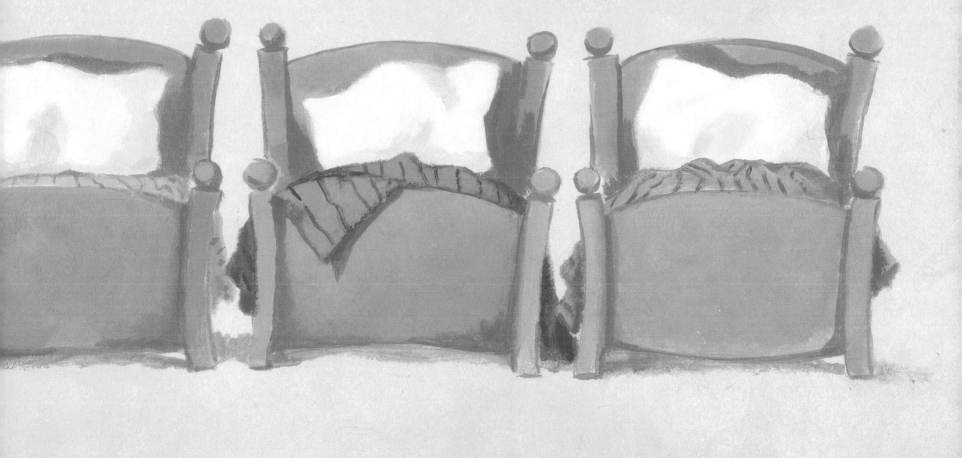

For every child who loves bears and for my amazing editor,
Sarah Ketchersid, who understands them
S. P.

Especially for Miss Catherine's pre-school class
D. W.

First published 2012 by Walker Books Ltd
87 Vauxhall Walk, London SE11 5HJ

This edition published 2013

2 4 6 8 10 9 7 5 3 1

Text © 2012 Shirley Parenteau
Illustrations © 2012 David Walker

The right of Shirley Parenteau and David Walker to be identified as
author and illustrator respectively of this work has been asserted by them
in accordance with the Copyright, Designs and Patents Act 1988

This book has been typeset in Journal

Printed in China

British Library Cataloguing in Publication Data:
a catalogue record for this book is available from the British Library

ISBN 978-1-4063-4503-2

www.walker.co.uk